Don't Hurt My Pony

Do you love ponies? Be a Pony Pal!

Look for these Pony Pal books:

#1 I Want a Pony

#2 A Pony for Keeps

#3 A Pony in Trouble

#4 Give Me Back My Pony

#5 Pony to the Rescue

#6 Too Many Ponies

#7 Runaway Pony

#8 Good-bye Pony

#9 The Wild Pony

Super Special #1 The Baby Pony

coming soon

#11 Circus Pony

Don't Hurt My Pony

Jeanne Betancourt

illustrated by Paul Bachem

SCHOLASTIC INC.
New York Toronto London Auckland Sydney

ISBN 0-590-62975-1

24 23 22 5 6 7 8 9/0

Printed in the U.S.A. 40

First Scholastic printing, July 1996

Thank you to Margaret Barney and
Shanna Barney for sharing their
knowledge of horses with me.

Contents

1.	Lulu's Present	1
2.	Surprise!	9
3.	The Search	17
4.	On Wheels	25
5.	In Hiding	34
6.	Three Ideas	42
7.	Trapped!	48
8.	The Chase	56
9.	Tell Me Why	63
10.	On the Porch	70

Don't Hurt My Pony

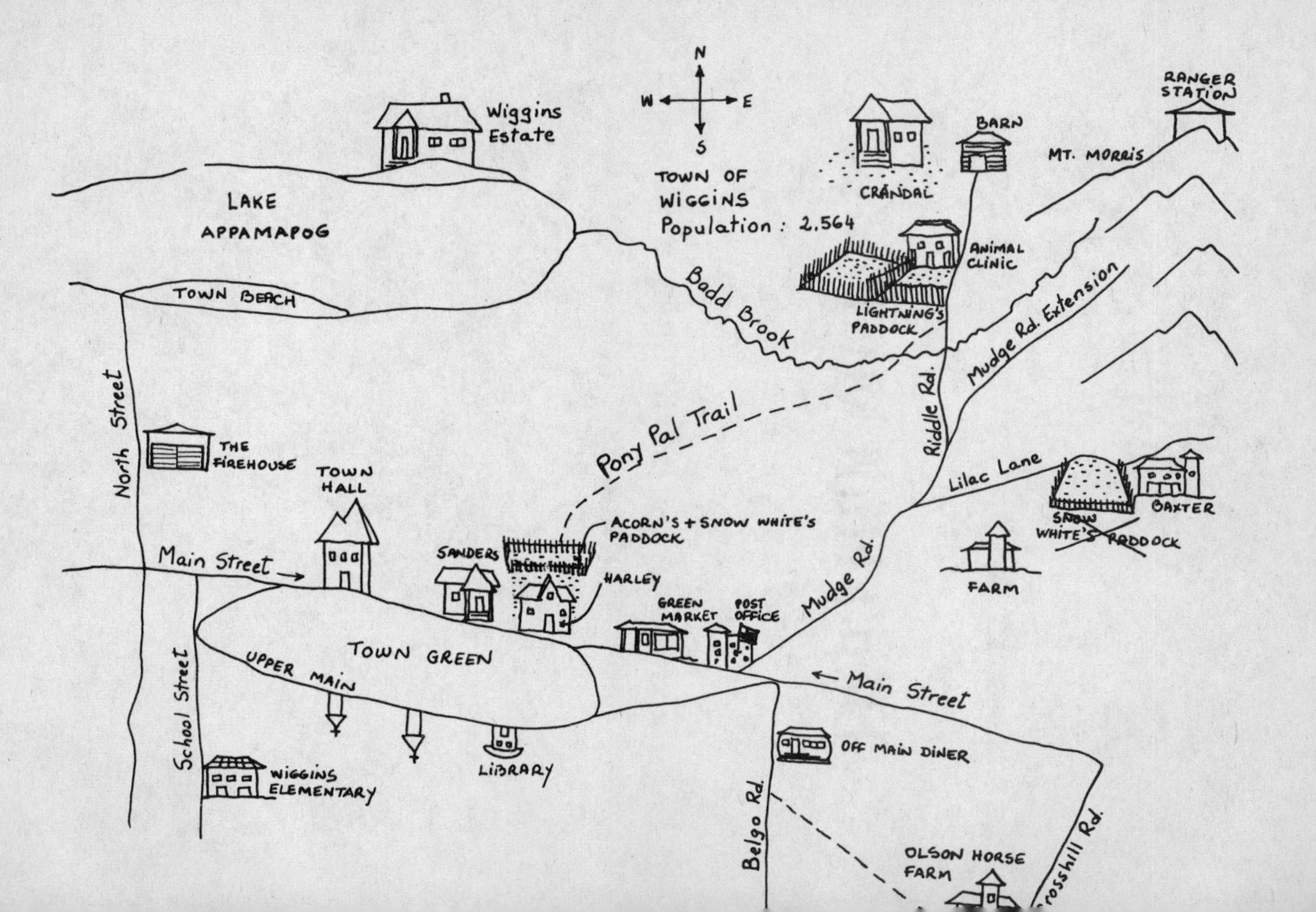

N
W
E
S
TOWN OF WIGGINS
Population : 2.564
Wiggins Estate
LAKE APPAMAPOG
TOWN BEACH
CRANDAL
BARN
RANGER STATION
MT. MORRIS
ANIMAL CLINIC
LIGHTNING'S PADDOCK
Badd Brook
Mudge Rd. Extension
Riddle Rd.
Pony Pal Trail
North Street
THE FIREHOUSE
TOWN HALL
Lilac Lane
BAXTER
SNOW WHITE'S PADDOCK
FARM
ACORN'S + SNOW WHITE'S PADDOCK
SANDERS
HARLEY
Main Street
Mudge Rd.
GREEN MARKET
POST OFFICE
TOWN GREEN
UPPER MAIN
Main Street
School Street
WIGGINS ELEMENTARY
LIBRARY
OFF MAIN DINER
Belgo Rd.
OLSON HORSE FARM
rosshill Rd.

Lulu's Present

Lulu Sanders was in the field with her pony, Snow White. She laid her head on the pony's side. "Dad's going to Africa to study elephants," she said. "And he won't let me go with him." She sniffed back tears. "It's not fair."

"Lulu," a voice said softly. Lulu looked up and saw her father. "I'm sorry you can't come with me," he said. "But this wouldn't be a fun trip for you. We'll be living in difficult conditions."

"I've been on hard trips with you before," said Lulu.

"There are lots of poachers where I'm going," Mr. Sanders said. "They're shooting the elephants for their tusks. It's too dangerous to bring you."

"I'd be careful," said Lulu.

"You're better off here with your grandmother," Lulu's father said. He stroked Snow White's neck. "Besides, you and Snow White are starting a three-day camping trip today. That's an adventure."

"It's not the same as tracking elephants and stopping those mean poachers," said Lulu.

"Everything you and your friends do seems to turn out to be an adventure," said Mr. Sanders. He took a small, black camera out of his pocket and handed it to Lulu. "This is for you," he said.

Lulu took the camera. She loved how it fit in the palm of her hand. "Thanks, Dad," she said.

"Take pictures of your camping trip," he

said. “Not just of your friends, but of the animals and plants that you see, too.”

“Just the way you do,” said Lulu.

Her father smiled. “We can share our pictures when I come home,” he said.

Snow White nudged Lulu’s shoulder gently and whinnied as if to say, “Take my picture.” Lulu and her father laughed. The first picture Lulu took with her new camera was of her father with his arm around Snow White.

After Lulu’s father left for the airport, Lulu saddled up Snow White for a trail ride to the campsite on the Wiggins estate. Her Pony Pals, Anna and Pam, had gone there early that morning to organize their supplies for the three-day stay in the woods.

Ms. Wiggins was a good friend of the Pony Pals and gave them permission to ride and to camp out on her land. She showed them the best campsite and lent them her tent. Lulu knew it made her grandmother and her father feel better that Ms. Wiggins promised to check on the Pony Pals during their camp out.

Lulu tied her rain gear to the front of her saddle and her sleeping bag to the back. Her clothes were already packed in the two saddlebags. Next, Lulu hung her red whistle around her neck and tucked her new camera in her saddlebag.

Grandmother Sanders came out to tell Lulu to be careful and to say good-bye. "This seems to be a day for good-byes," her Grandmother said.

Lulu swung up into the saddle. "I'll see you tonight, Grandma," said Lulu. "You're coming to our campsite for supper. Remember?"

Grandmother frowned. She didn't like outdoor living as much as Lulu and her father did. "I'd much rather take you girls out for a nice dinner at the diner," Grandmother said. "But I'll be there around six o'clock."

Lulu rode Snow White through the gate and onto Pony Pal Trail. She still wished she were headed to Africa with her father. Lulu's mother died when Lulu was four years old, so she especially missed her father when he was on one of his business trips.

At the three birch trees, Lulu turned Snow White left onto the Wiggins estate. She saw a rabbit sitting by the side of the trail. Before the rabbit noticed her, Lulu snapped its picture. As the bunny hopped away, Lulu thought, It would be so much more exciting to be taking pictures of elephants!

Lulu and Snow White reached Badd Brook. Lulu dismounted to give Snow White a rest and a drink. While Snow White drank, Lulu read the animal tracks in the mud at the edge of the brook. It had rained the night before, so Lulu knew that the fresh tracks had been made that morning. She figured out that two fawns and an adult deer had been there. Near a big rock Lulu recognized a set of raccoon tracks. And on the other side of the rock there were

tracks that were made by a fox. Lulu took pictures of the tracks.

Lulu led her pony across the brook. She mounted Snow White again. Lulu couldn't wait to tell Anna and Pam about the tracks she'd seen. She'd show them her new camera, too. "Let's go find our Pony Pals," she told Snow White. They faced an open stretch of trail. Lulu tapped Snow White's side with her heels. Snow White smoothly moved into a trot and then a canter.

Suddenly Snow White stopped and pawed the ground. "Keep going," Lulu said. But Snow White just pulled against the reins and made a low snort that said "No." Lulu looked down to see if there was an animal hole in their path. There wasn't. Maybe Snow White just wanted to eat grass. Lulu tugged at the reins to bring Snow White's head up. "You can graze at the campsite," she said. "Now let's go."

Through the reins, Lulu could feel that Snow White didn't want to go forward. But she knew that it was important for her to be in charge of her pony. She tapped Snow White's side with her heels and said sternly, "Behave yourself, Snow White." Snow White finally moved forward. But after a few steps the pony stumbled. Lulu could feel that something was wrong with one of Snow White's legs. She jumped off her pony and spoke calmly to Snow White. "Good girl," she said. "Good pony." Snow White made a frightened whinny.

Lulu was frightened, too. What had happened to her pony? Had she sprained or broken a leg? Then Lulu saw what was wrong. A metal animal trap was clamped tight on Snow White's front right hoof.

Surprise!

Lulu studied the metal trap on Snow White's hoof. It was clamped down on the front part of the hoof and wasn't hurting her leg. Lulu grabbed the edges of the trap and pulled as hard as she could. The trap sprung open and Snow White lifted out her hoof. Lulu held the reins and watched Snow White take a few steps. She wasn't limping, but she was acting frightened.

"Snow White, you were spooked because something was wrong on the trail," Lulu told her frightened pony. “I thought you wanted to eat grass. I’m sorry.”

Lulu looked closely at the place where the trap had been hidden. She noticed dried blood sprinkled there. Whoever set the trap used dried blood as a lure to attract meat-eating animals. But ponies don’t eat meat and don’t like the smell of blood, thought Lulu. That’s why Snow White was spooked.

Lulu wondered what animal the trapper was trying to catch. Was it the raccoon whose prints she’d seen in the mud? Or maybe the fox. “No one is going to trap raccoon or fox with this trap,” Lulu told Snow White. She put the trap in her saddlebag on top of the first aid kit.

Snow White tugged on the reins and whinnied. She was more spooked than ever. “Okay, Snow White,” Lulu said. “We’ll go. This place is giving me the creeps, too.”

Lulu wished that Anna and Pam were there. She wanted to tell them what happened to Snow White and decide what they should do about the poacher. She remembered her whistle. She could blow one short, one long, and one short blast for an SOS signal. Then she thought, What if there are more traps along the trails? I don't want Acorn and Lightning to get caught in a trap the way Snow White did. Someone could get badly hurt. Lulu didn't blow the SOS signal.

Snow White nickered nervously. "I'm going to walk to the campsite with you instead of riding," Lulu told Snow White. "That way I can look for more traps and you'll be safe." Lulu looked into her pony's eyes. "Don't worry, Snow White," she said. "I'll protect you."

As Lulu led Snow White along the trails she thought about her Pony Pals. She'd been friends with Anna and Pam only since the fall when she moved to Wiggins. But sometimes Lulu felt like she'd known Anna and Pam all her life.

Lulu's grandmother's house was right

next door to Anna Harley's house. The Harleys had a paddock behind their backyard that Snow White and Acorn shared. Lulu loved having Anna and Acorn as neighbors. They were both smart and full of fun.

The paddock that Acorn and Snow White shared was connected to Pam Crandal's place by Pony Pal Trail. The Pony Pals used the mile-and-a-half woodland trail to go back and forth to one another's houses.

Pam Crandal and Anna Harley had been best friends since kindergarten. The two friends were very different from one another. Anna, who was dyslexic, didn't like to read and write. But she was a terrific artist and loved to draw and paint. Pam loved to read and write. But she wasn't a very good artist. Pam liked to plan ahead, while Anna liked surprises. But Pam and Anna had one big thing in common. They both loved ponies and knew a lot about them. And so did Lulu. Lulu felt lucky to have such wonderful friends and to be a Pony Pal.

Lulu walked slowly along the trails so she could look for traps. She didn't find any more. But Lulu knew there could be traps in the woods between the trails. Lulu and Snow White made a right turn. They walked carefully along a very narrow trail until they finally came to a clearing. Ms. Wiggins' blue tent was set up under a pine tree at one edge of the clearing. The rest of the clearing was fenced in to make a corral. Acorn and Lightning were grazing in the corral. Snow White whinnied happily to them. Acorn and Lightning called back to her. Lightning and Acorn ran to the gate to meet Snow White.

"We're here!" Lulu shouted. "Anna! Pam! Where are you?" No one answered her call.

Lulu took off Snow White's saddle and bridle and put her in the corral with the other ponies. Next, she hung her saddle on a branch of the hickory tree next to Pam's and Anna's saddles. Then she put her sleeping bag and supplies in the tent. Anna's and Pam's sleeping bags and supplies were already there. But where were Anna and Pam?

Lulu checked the time on her watch. It had taken her a long time to reach the campsite. Had Anna and Pam been worried and gone looking for her in the woods? Lulu had to find them and warn them about the traps. She had to tell them that someone was poaching on the Wiggins estate.

Suddenly hands clamped over Lulu's eyes from behind. Was it the poacher? Lulu yanked her head away from the hands and turned around.

"Surprise!" shouted Anna and Pam. Anna handed Lulu a bouquet of wildflowers. "We know you're sad about your dad leaving, so we picked you flowers and brought a special lunch from the diner," said Pam. "We'll eat it by the stream."

Anna held out a take-out bag from her mother's diner. "Tuna sandwiches on rolls, fruit salad, and brownies," she said.

Lulu's heart was still pounding hard from being frightened. "Thank you," she said in a shaky voice.

"Are you all right?" Pam asked Lulu. "You look funny."

"You scared me," said Lulu. "I thought you were the poacher."

"Poacher?" asked Anna. "What are you talking about?"

Lulu handed the flowers back to Anna and said, "I'll show you." She took the trap out of her saddlebag and held it up. "Someone set this trap on Ms. Wiggins' land," she told them. "And we have to find out who did it."

The Search

The Pony Pals ate their picnic by the stream and talked about the poaching.

"Someone was trapping illegally on our property when I was little," said Pam. "My mom told me about it. People are supposed to get permission to trap from the property owner. Add there's a law that you have to put a name tag on every trap you put out."

"There wasn't a name tag on the trap I found," said Lulu.

"Ms. Wiggins would never give permission to trap on her land," added Anna.

"My mom and dad didn't give permission either," said Pam.

"So what happened?" asked Anna.

"Trappers check their traps early in the morning," said Pam. "My dad caught this man. He had to pay a fine and promise not to trap illegally again."

"What animals was the man trapping?" asked Lulu.

"Fox," answered Pam. "Trappers can sell a fox pelt for a lot of money."

"What's a *pelt*?" asked Anna.

"An animal's skin and fur," said Pam.

Anna frowned. Lulu remembered the fox and raccoon tracks she'd seen by Badd Brook. Maybe she saved one of those animals from being trapped.

"What do we do now?" Pam asked. "Should we go tell Ms. Wiggins?"

"I think we should try to figure out who's setting traps before we tell anyone anything," said Lulu.

"But we should put the trap back," said

Anna. "If we leave it closed it won't hurt any animals."

"Then in the morning we can spy and see who comes to check it," added Lulu.

"We should hunt for more traps, too," said Pam.

"Snow White can help us," said Lulu. "She's great at sniffing out traps."

The girls finished the brownies and cleaned up from their picnic. Then they walked through the woods back to the campsite. Lulu put her bottle of water, her first aid kit, a flashlight, and a couple of carrots in her backpack. She haltered Snow White, and the Pony Pals were ready.

They went back to where Lulu and Snow White found the trap. Suddenly Snow White pulled on her lead rope. "We're almost where Snow White was trapped this morning," said Lulu. "It's right around the next turn."

"She's spooked again," said Pam. "She must smell that dried blood."

"I'll stay with her, Lulu," said Anna. "You can show Pam where the trap was."

Lulu showed Pam the spot on the trail where Snow White stepped into the trap. Pam pointed to a big stick lying nearby. "I bet the trap was behind that stick," she said. "Trappers put a stick in front of the trap. Then when an animal steps over the stick its foot lands in the trap."

Lulu placed the closed trap on the other side of the stick. Pam covered it with pine needles.

Pam and Lulu looked around for a good hiding place for them to use the next morning. Lulu pointed to a big clump of honeysuckle bushes. "How about behind those bushes?" she asked. The two girls checked that there was enough space behind the bushes for three people to fit.

"Pam. Lulu," Anna called. "Come here." Lulu heard Snow White snorting.

Pam and Lulu left the bushes and ran back to Anna and Snow White. Snow White was backing away from the woods. "I think she smells something in there," said Anna.

Lulu sniffed. "I do, too," she said.

Pam stayed with Snow White while Anna and Lulu went into the woods. Lulu sniffed and sniffed. Her nose led her to a big rotted-out log. The two girls squatted down and looked inside the log. "I think I see something shiny in there," said Anna. "I bet it's a trap."

Lulu put her hand over her nose. "And I *smell* a dead fish," she said. Lulu took the flashlight out of her backpack and moved the beam around inside the log. "There *is* a trap in there," she told Anna.

"Don't put your hand in that log," said Anna. "You might be caught by the trap."

Lulu picked up a stick and handed it to Anna. "Maybe we can get it with this," she said. Lulu lit up the inside of the log with the flashlight while Anna poked inside with the stick. "I've got it!" Anna exclaimed. "I caught the trap." She pulled the stick out of the log. A trap was clamped to the end.

Lulu and Anna told Pam about the trap and the dead fish lure. "Trappers use smelly stuff to attract raccoons," Pam said.

Lulu stayed with Snow White while Pam and Anna went back into the woods to put the trap back in the log and cover up their tracks. While they waited, Lulu gave Snow White a carrot. "You did good work," she said. "You smelled that fish lure."

After Snow White ate the carrot she started fidgeting and pawing the ground with her front foot. "What's wrong?" asked Lulu. "Do you smell another trap?" Just then Anna and Pam came running toward them. Anna motioned Lulu to be quiet. "Someone's coming," Pam whispered. "We heard them."

"So did Snow White," said Lulu.

"Let's hide," suggested Anna.

Snow White snorted. The girls looked at her. How could they hide with a pony? Especially a white one.

The Pony Pals heard laughter and talking in the distance. The voices were coming closer.

"Do you think it's the poachers?" asked Anna.

"It could be," said Lulu.

"Let's run," said Pam. "Lulu, you can ride bareback."

"If we run, it'll look like we've been up to something," said Anna.

"Like messing with traps," added Lulu.

The voices were closer now. Snow White whinnied nervously. The three girls held their breaths and waited to see who was coming toward them on the trail.

On Wheels

Two boys on mountain bikes sped down the trail toward the Pony Pals.

"It's Tommy Rand," said Pam.

"With Mike Lacey," added Lulu.

"What are *they* doing here?" said Anna.

Tommy Rand and Mike Lacey were eighth graders at Wiggins Elementary. The two boys often acted mean, especially to kids younger than them. The Pony Pals knew Mike's younger sister, Rosalie. They liked Rosalie. But they *did not* like her brother Mike.

Lulu could see that Tommy and Mike were startled when they first saw a big white animal on the trail. But when they realized it was just a pony, they kept coming toward the three girls. Snow White was spooked by the speeding bikes. Lulu pulled her off the trail to calm her down.

Tommy and Mike rode right by the Pony Pals, then skidded their bikes around to face them. Dead leaves and twigs blew in Lulu's face. She wondered what the Terrible Twosome were doing on the Wiggins estate.

"Hey, Mike," Tommy said. "I think I just saw some strange *bugs*."

"You mean *bugs* like *pests*?" asked Mike.

"Yeah," answered Tommy. He squinted his eyes as if he had trouble seeing the girls. "Oh, I see," he exclaimed. "It's the *Pony Pests*."

"I guess the *Pony Pests* ride their little ponies around here," said Mike.

"Their little *pesty* ponies," added Tommy. He reached out his hand to pat Snow White.

Snow White snorted at him. Tommy pulled back his hand.

"You leave my pony alone," Lulu told him.

"Who's touching your stupid pony?" asked Tommy.

"You guys are such jerks," mumbled Anna.

"This is private property," said Pam. "You're not supposed to be here."

"There are No Trespassing signs all over the place," said Lulu.

"So how come the Pony Pests are here?" asked Mike.

"We have permission," Lulu answered.

"From Ms. Wiggins," added Anna. "She's our friend."

"We got permission, too," said Tommy. "Ms. Wiggins said we could ride our bikes here anytime we wanted."

"I don't believe she said that," said Anna.

"Me either," said Pam.

"So don't believe," said Tommy. "Who cares?"

"Let's go, Tommy," Mike said, "before I fall asleep from boredom." He turned his bike around.

Tommy reared up on his back wheel, and the Terrible Twosome took off.

Dust blew in the Pony Pals' faces. Snow White snorted. Tommy and Mike pedaled out of sight.

"I hate those boys," said Lulu. She gave Snow White another carrot so the pony would forget about being spooked by bikes.

"I'm glad our campsite is on the other side of the mansion," said Pam. "They'll never find us over there."

"First animal traps, now Tommy and Mike on those bikes," said Anna.

"Do you think Ms. Wiggins really said they could ride their bikes on her estate?" asked Lulu.

"She lets people hike and bird-watch here," Anna said.

"And she told the Monroes they could drive their horse-drawn buggy on the trails," added Pam.

"But Mike and Tommy are such jerks," said Lulu. "She'd never let them ride here."

"Maybe she doesn't know they're jerks," said Pam.

"Then we'll tell her," said Anna. "When we tell her about the poachers."

"Do you think we should tell Mike and Tommy about the poachers?" asked Pam. "They might step in a trap or something."

"If they got hurt, we'd probably be the ones who'd have to go get help," said Lulu.

"I bet if Tommy Rand was hurt he'd be a big baby," said Anna. The girls giggled.

"But that would be the end of our camping trip," said Pam.

The Pony Pals decided that if they saw Tommy and Mike again, they'd warn them about the traps.

"Maybe we won't see them again," said Pam.

"I hope not," said Lulu.

A few minutes later the girls heard laughter and hoots on the trail. "They're back," said Anna.

"They're noisy, but they won't hurt you," Lulu told Snow White.

It looked like the two boys would ride right past the Pony Pals. So Anna yelled, "STOP!"

Tommy and Mike skidded their bikes to a stop. Pam spoke before Tommy could make one of his silly Pony Pest jokes. "Someone has been setting animal traps in the woods," she said. "You should be careful."

Tommy pretended to be alarmed. "You mean someone is catching the baby bunnies and the sweet squirrels," he said.

"And the friendly foxes," added Mike.

"Maybe *we* should do that," joked Tommy. "Then we could have rabbit stew for dinner."

The Pony Pals didn't say another word to those boys. They turned their backs on them and started on down the trail. Tommy and Mike didn't care. They got back on their bikes and rode off in the opposite direction. Lulu could hear that they were still making stupid animal jokes.

"We shouldn't have bothered to warn them," said Anna.

"It's just like them to make jokes about someone trapping poor innocent animals," said Pam.

Lulu looked at her watch. "It's five o'clock," she said. "Let's go back to our campsite."

Lulu's grandmother came to the campsite for dinner that night. Everyone had a good time. The girls didn't mention the traps they'd discovered in the woods.

After Grandmother left, the Pony Pals crawled into their tent and closed the flap. Pam hung her lit flashlight on a tent rope and the girls sat on their sleeping bags.

"I hope that we find that poacher tomorrow," Lulu said.

"Me too," said Anna.

"At least we won't find any trapped animals," said Pam.

"What if there are more traps?" asked Lulu. "What if we didn't discover them all?"

"I hope we did," said Anna. "It must be awful to be caught in one of those things."

"We better go to sleep," said Pam. "We have to wake up early tomorrow morning."

The girls crawled into their sleeping bags, said good night to one another, and stopped talking. But Lulu lay awake for a long time. She was wondering what they would find along the trails and in the woods the next day.

In Hiding

The beeping of Lulu's watch alarm woke her up. She opened her eyes and saw she was in a small, dark space. For an instant, Lulu wondered where she was. As she turned off her alarm, she remembered. She was in a tent on a camping trip with Pam and Anna.

Pam's voice came from the sleeping bag beside her. "Is it time?" she asked.

"Uh-huh," answered Lulu sleepily.

Anna came into the tent. She beamed the flashlight at Pam and Lulu. "Morning, sleepyheads," she said. "I already put out fresh water for the ponies and filled a water bottle for us. Let's go."

Lulu and Pam crawled out of their sleeping bags. The Pony Pals had slept in their clothes. Lulu hung her whistle around her neck. They were ready to spy on the poacher.

When Lulu came out of the tent, the first thing she saw in the early morning light was the glow of Snow White's coat. Lulu went to the fence to say good morning to her pony. Snow White came over and made a low whinny, as if to say, "Can I come with you?"

"I can't take you spying," Lulu said. "You're too hard to hide."

In the dawn's light the woods looked mysterious and beautiful. The Pony Pals saw a fox streak across the trail ahead of them. A little later they heard a cracking of small branches in the woods. The girls stopped in their tracks. Was it the poacher? Lulu saw the white flash of a deer's tail. "It was just a deer," she whispered to Anna and Pam.

By the time the Pony Pals reached their hiding place near the trap, the sun was up. They stood close together behind the big honeysuckle bush. Lulu took a pad and pencil out of her pocket. From now on if they wanted to say something they'd write it down.

After a while Lulu heard the mumble of voices in the distance. She wrote on the pad:

There are two of them. I think they are checking the trap in the log.

Soon the voices were closer. Lulu could tell that Pam and Anna were as nervous and scared as she was.

Lulu thought she heard, "Fox . . . dollars . . . better than raccoon." And another voice saying, "Why . . . traps . . . broken." Even though she heard only parts of sentences, Lulu recognized the voices. She scribbled on the pad again.

TOMMY and MIKE!

Anna and Pam nodded.

Lulu peeked through the leaves of the bush. She watched the boys ride their bikes straight to the trap. Tommy had an empty canvas sack slung over his shoulder. Lulu knew it was for carrying the animals they killed. She was glad that the bag was empty.

The boys stopped at the trap, hopped off their bikes, and dropped them to the ground. Mike uncovered the trap. "We didn't catch anything in this trap either," he said. "It's closed, but it's empty."

"We haven't caught nothin'," said Tommy. "Not even a rabbit. I thought you knew how to trap, Mike."

"I do," Mike said. "I told you. My dad taught me."

Tommy held up the trap. "Your dad's traps are lousy," he said.

Mike grabbed the trap from Tommy. "Hey, watch what you say about my dad."

"Yeah, yeah," said Tommy.

Mike reset the trap, covered it with dried leaves, and laid a stick behind it. Then he pointed straight at the bushes. The Pony Pals exchanged terrified looks. Had Mike seen them? They held their breaths.

"I bet the fox has a den near those bushes," Mike told Tommy. "I'll put the stick on that side of the trap."

"Sure. Okay. Fine," grumbled Tommy.

Mike stood up. "That's the last trap," he said. "Let's go. We'll check on the traps again late this afternoon."

The two boys got on their bikes and rode away.

The Pony Pals stayed behind the bushes for a few minutes after the boys left. Finally, Anna whispered, "I didn't think kids could trap."

"They're not supposed to," said Pam. "It's against the law."

"So they broke two laws," said Lulu. "They are too young to trap and they put traps on private land without permission."

"Let's go fix the traps so none of them work again," said Anna.

The Pony Pals came out from their hiding place. Pam poked the trap with the stick that Mike had just set. The trap clamped tight on the stick.

As the girls set off other traps, they discussed what to do about Tommy and Mike.

"We better tell Ms. Wiggins," said Pam.

"Should we report Mike and Tommy to the police *before* we tell Ms. Wiggins?" asked Lulu.

"I think we should tell their parents first," said Anna. "Mrs. Lacey is strict. She'll punish Mike for sure."

"Wait a minute," said Lulu. "We're forgetting one very important thing."

"What?" asked Pam and Anna.

"We don't have any *proof* that Tommy and Mike are the poachers," she said.

"Of course we do," said Anna. "We *saw* them."

"That's just our word against theirs," said Lulu. "We need more evidence than that."

"Lulu's right," said Pam. "But how are we going to get evidence?"

"They're not checking on the traps until later," said Pam. "We have all day to think of what to do."

"It's time for three ideas," said Anna.

Three Ideas

The Pony Pals returned to their campsite. They fed their ponies, made breakfast for themselves, and cleaned up. Then they saddled up their ponies for a trail ride up Great View Hill. All that time Lulu wondered how they could prove that Tommy and Mike were the poachers. Finally she had an idea she thought was good. She wrote it down before she mounted Snow White for the trail ride.

The Pony Pals rode to the top of Great View Hill. They dismounted, gave their ponies apples, and tied their lead ropes to a tree. Then the girls sat on a big rock. They had a bird's eye view of the Wiggins estate. Lulu could see the Wiggins mansion and all the paths that led to it through the woods.

"Look," said Pam. "There's our blue tent."

"It's great up here," said Anna.

Pam passed around boxes of juice.

"Who wants to show their idea first?" asked Anna.

"I do," answered Lulu. She unfolded her paper and put it out on the rock in front of them.

Take pictures of Mike and Tommy
Checking the traps.

"That's a great idea," said Anna. "Detectives take pictures for evidence all the time. You can use your new camera."

"Mike and Tommy said they would check the traps later today," said Lulu. "We can

go to the same hiding place and take pictures from there."

"What's your idea, Anna?" asked Pam.

Anna put a piece of paper on the rock next to Lulu's idea.

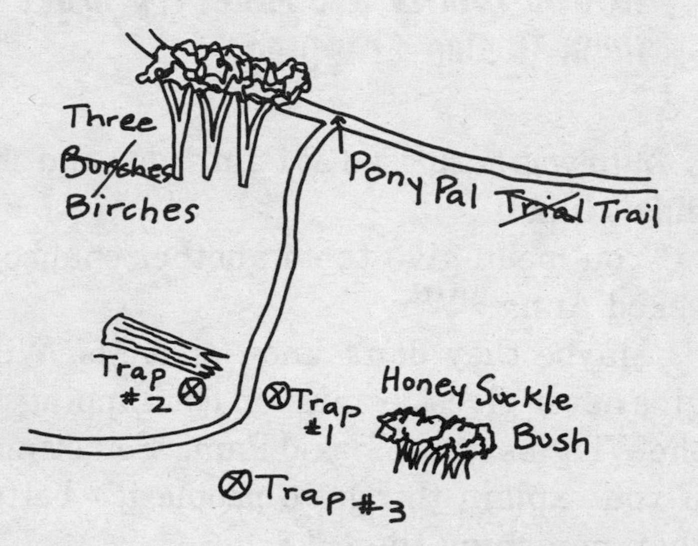

"Terrific," said Lulu. "What a good idea!"

"This will show the police and Ms. Wiggins that we know where all the traps are," said Anna.

"What's your idea, Pam?" Lulu asked.

"My idea isn't about gathering evidence," said Pam. "I thought about something we could do *instead* of turning Mike and Tommy in." Pam handed her idea to Lulu. Lulu read it out aloud.

Talk to Tommy and Mike. Try to get them to stop trapping.

Lulu was surprised at Pam's idea and she didn't like it.

"You mean give them another chance?" asked Anna. "Why?"

"Maybe they don't know that Ms. Wiggins never gives permission for trapping on the Wiggins estate," said Pam. "Sometimes if you explain things to people it's better than punishing them."

"Tommy and Mike already set those traps," said Lulu. "They know that what they're doing is wrong. That's why they did it. I think they should be punished."

"Me too," said Anna. "Those guys are always acting mean. This is a great chance to teach them a lesson."

"And save some innocent animals," said Lulu.

"They might say they'd stop just so we wouldn't turn them in," said Anna.

"And then just go off and trap illegally someplace else," added Lulu.

"I didn't think of that," said Pam. She smiled at her friends. "But I still wish we could give them a chance to stop poaching on their own."

Lulu thought, I'm not giving Tommy and Mike a second chance.

Lulu stood up. "What they did is wrong," she said. "We have to turn them in.

Trapped!

The Pony Pals rode down Great View Hill. "What are we going to do till it's time to spy on Mike and Tommy again?" asked Anna.

"Let's have a picnic near the falls on Badd Brook," said Lulu.

"And forget about Mike and Tommy," said Pam.

The girls went back to their campsite and packed a picnic lunch. Then they rode over to the waterfalls on Badd Brook. Their ponies drank from the brook and grazed on the grass beside it.

"I think our ponies like this spot as much as we do," Lulu said. Pam and Anna agreed as they watched the playful ponies. The girls ate their picnic near the brook. Then they took off their shoes and rolled up their jeans. Lulu dangled her feet in the cold water and listened to the water tumbling over the rocks.

"Look, it's the Pony Pests and their pesty ponies!" a loud voice said. Lulu looked up. Mike and Tommy were walking toward them. "Maybe the Pony Pests live in these woods," said Tommy.

"They'd be too scared," said Mike.

Lulu was glad that those boys didn't know that they *were* living in the woods for three days.

"Do you think they've already checked the traps?" Anna whispered to Lulu.

"Mike said 'late afternoon,' " Lulu told her. "It's only two-thirty."

Tommy picked up a small flat stone. So did Mike.

"There are lots of wonderful animals in these woods," Pam told the boys. "Have you seen any?"

"Sure," said Tommy. "Lots." He squatted near a still pool of water at the edge of the brook. He skipped a stone over the water and counted the times it hopped. "One. Two." He turned to Mike and said, "Top that."

Mike skipped a stone and counted. "One. Two. Three. I beat you," he told Tommy.

"Your stone was smoother than mine," said Tommy.

"Ms. Wiggins doesn't let anyone hunt or trap in these woods," Pam said. "She loves all the animals and wants to protect them." Lulu was afraid that Pam was going to tell the boys that she knew they were trapping.

Tommy imitated a girl's voice and repeated what Pam said. " 'She loves all the animals and wants to protect them,' " he teased.

Mike laughed.

"This place has loads of deer," said Tommy.

"I went deer hunting with my dad once," Mike said. "Venison is great eating."

Tommy imitated a girl again. "Oh, no, you killed an innocent little deer?"

Mike laughed again.

"I'm a great shot with rabbits," Tommy bragged. He held up an imaginary gun and shouted, "Pow! Pow! Pow!"

"You guys are disgusting," said Pam. She walked away from them and sat down on a rock to put on her boots. Anna and Lulu followed her. It was time for an emergency meeting of the Pony Pals.

The boys continued their game of Skip a Stone on the Water.

"I hate those boys," whispered Anna.

"It's bad enough we have to go to school with them," said Pam. "I hate seeing them here."

Tommy shouted "Yes!" and threw a fist in the air. "I made three skips, man. Now watch me get four."

"They'll probably check the traps when they get sick of skipping stones and bothering us," said Lulu.

"We don't have time to bring our ponies back to the corral," said Pam.

"How can we spy on them with three ponies?" asked Anna.

"I'll stay here with the ponies," said Pam, "while you two do the detective work. Tommy and Mike will think we're here the whole time."

The girls went back to the edge of the brook where Tommy and Mike were skipping stones. "One. Two," counted Mike. "The water's too rough there."

Lulu picked up a flat stone. She skimmed it in the same spot Mike had used. Anna and Pam counted. "One. Two. Three."

"Big deal," said Tommy.

Lulu picked up another stone. She leveled it over the water and let it go with a flick of her wrist. "One. Two. Three. Four," counted Anna and Pam.

"Just luck," said Mike.

"Let's get out of here," said Tommy. "The Pony Pests are getting on my nerves."

After the boys left, Anna and Lulu checked Anna's Map of Traps. "There are two traps between here and where we'll be hiding," Anna said. "They'll check those first."

"Be careful," Pam warned.

Anna and Lulu snuck around the field, along a narrow trail through the woods, and hid behind a bush. Lulu parted two branches and looked through her camera lens. "That'll be perfect," Lulu whispered. She took a deep breath. "Now all we have to do is wait."

A few minutes later Anna and Lulu heard the boys coming toward them. "Man," said Tommy, "we haven't trapped one animal. This is the dumbest idea you ever had."

They got off their bikes. Tommy reached over and picked up the trap with the stick in its jaws. "How much money do you think we'll get for a *stick* pelt?" he asked disgustedly.

Lulu pushed the button on the camera. Suddenly, the bright light of the camera's flash lit up the woods.

"What's that?" shouted Mike.

"Someone's in that bush," yelled Tommy.

"They see us," Anna whispered.

"Run!" said Lulu.

The Chase

"It's those girls!" Mike shouted. "They were taking pictures of us trapping."

As Lulu and Anna ran, they heard Tommy and Mike running through the woods behind them.

"Let's get them!" yelled Tommy.

Lulu and Anna knew their way around the Wiggins estate better than Tommy and Mike. And because the girls were smaller than the boys, they could move faster through the dense part of the woods.

Lulu and Anna came to the beginning of a trail.

"I have an idea," Lulu said. "Give me your headband. Quick."

Anna removed her blue headband and handed it to Lulu. Lulu went a few feet up the trail and dropped it. "They'll think we went that way," she explained.

"Good thinking," said Anna.

The two girls left the trail and moved quietly through the woods. When they heard the boys' voices, they stayed perfectly still and listened.

"Hey man, look," said Tommy. "They dropped something."

"That means they went on this trail," said Mike. "Let's go."

The boys were following Lulu's false clue. Anna and Lulu hit a silent high five.

"Now let's go back to Pam and the ponies," said Anna.

"What's the fastest way to the waterfall?" asked Lulu.

Anna pointed to a hill to their left. "Badd Brook is on the other side of that hill," she said.

"We can take a shortcut over the top of the hill," said Lulu.

"Then we can follow the brook to the falls," added Anna. "Let's go."

As Lulu and Anna were climbing the hill, Anna started giggling.

"What's so funny?" asked Lulu.

"Guess where the trail ends that Tommy and Mike took?"

Lulu thought for a second. Then she giggled, too. "At Ms. Wiggins' house," she said.

"Yes!" said Anna. "Won't they be surprised!"

When Lulu and Anna reached the top of the hill, Lulu looked behind her. She had a view of the trail cutting through the woods and she saw Tommy and Mike running along it. But something was wrong. Tommy and Mike were running *away* from Ms. Wiggins' house!

Lulu dropped to the ground and pulled Anna beside her. "Stay down," she told her. "Tommy and Mike figured out we tricked them. They're coming back."

The girls scrambled down the other side of the rocky hill. They found Badd Brook and heard the rushing sound of the waterfalls. They walked along the edge of the brook. Soon they saw Pam and their ponies.

Pam saw them, too, and waved.

When Anna and Lulu reached Pam, they were out of breath.

"What happened?" asked Pam.

"Mike and Tommy . . . know . . . we were spying on them," said Anna.

"They're chasing us," added Lulu. She took a deep breath. "We all have to hide."

"How?" asked Pam. "We've got the ponies."

"Let's go to Ms. Wiggins' house," said Anna.

"But Tommy and Mike are on that trail," said Lulu.

"If we go through the big field," said

Pam, "we can pick up the trail farther along."

"We better hurry," said Lulu.

The three girls tightened their saddle girths, and pulled down their stirrups.

Lulu hid her camera in the inside pocket of her jacket. Then the Pony Pals led their ponies to the edge of the field and mounted them. "We need your help, Snow White," Lulu told her pony. She tapped Snow White's side with her heels. "We have to go *fast.*"

The three ponies galloped across the field. When they reached the trail, Lulu took the lead. Anna was behind her and Pam took up the rear. The trail was too twisty for galloping, but Snow White kept to a fast trot. We're going to make it, Lulu thought. Mike and Tommy won't catch us.

Just then, Lulu heard Pam shouting. At first she couldn't hear what Pam was saying. But when Anna repeated it she got the message. "The guys are catching up. They're on their bikes."

Mike and Tommy went back for their bikes, thought Lulu. She shifted her weight to tell Snow White to gallop again. "Snow White, you can go faster than a bike," she whispered. *"Go."*

Lulu felt her pony gather up and rush forward. She heard the quick hoofbeats of Acorn and Lightning behind them. Lulu didn't know if a pony could go faster than a mountain bike. She just hoped so.

Tell Me Why

Lulu directed Snow White around a wide turn in the trail.

"Lulu, they're catching up," Anna called.

"Come on, Snow White," Lulu said. "Don't let Mike and Tommy catch us." Lulu didn't look back. She focused on going forward. At the end of the turn, the trail opened to a large field. And beyond that field Lulu saw the Wiggins mansion.

The girls galloped side by side across the field. Lulu saw a woman standing at the far end. The woman noticed the riders and their ponies and waved. It was Ms. Wiggins! Lulu looked back toward the trail. The boys weren't following them anymore.

"We made it!" Anna shouted.

"What a ride!" exclaimed Pam.

"Thank you, Snow White," said Lulu. "You were great."

The Pony Pals slowed down their ponies and rode toward Ms. Wiggins. Lulu saw that she was painting at her outdoor easel.

When they reached her, Ms. Wiggins noticed the sweat on the ponies. "My goodness," she said. "You've worked your ponies hard."

"We better sponge them," said Lulu. "And give them some water after they cool down."

"You look like you could use something to drink yourselves," said Ms. Wiggins.

"We had to ride fast, Ms. Wiggins," said Anna.

"What's happened?" asked Ms. Wiggins. "Did something go wrong at your campsite?"

The girls dismounted. “Everything’s okay at the campsite,” said Lulu. “But someone’s been poaching on your land.”

Ms. Wiggins looked upset. “Illegal trappers,” she said. “I’ve had that problem before. I want you to tell me everything you’ve seen out there. But first take care of your ponies. I’ll pack up my paints and meet you at the house. We’ll have a cold drink and you can tell me what you know.”

Half an hour later the three girls were sitting on the front porch of the Wiggins mansion drinking lemonade. Their ponies were in the paddock with Ms. Wiggins’ horse, Picasso, and her driving pony, Beauty.

Lulu told Ms. Wiggins how Snow White was caught in a trap. Anna showed her the Map of Traps and Pam described how they set off the traps so no animals would be hurt.

“I can’t let you girls ride and camp around here if people are trapping,” said Ms. Wiggins. “I wonder who’s doing it?”

"We know who's doing it," said Lulu. "We spied on them."

"It's Tommy Rand and Mike Lacey," said Anna.

"I gave Mike Lacey permission to ride his mountain bike on the trails," said Ms. Wiggins. "Are you sure it's him?" Ms. Wiggins seemed really disappointed in Mike.

"Him and Tommy Rand," said Anna.

Lulu held up her camera. "I took a picture," she said. "For you and the police. It's evidence."

"They have no respect for wildlife," said Pam.

"And they don't respect people, either," added Anna.

"They're mean," said Lulu.

Lulu turned the camera over in her hand. "Should we tell the police before or after we have the film developed?" she asked.

Suddenly Anna jumped up and shouted, "Look!"

Lulu looked across the field. Two boys on bikes were riding toward the mansion.

“It’s them,” said Pam.

“Good,” said Ms. Wiggins. “Now we can hear their side of the story.”

The Pony Pals looked at one another. Didn’t Ms. Wiggins believe them?

Ms. Wiggins stood up and walked to the porch stairs to meet Mike and Tommy. “Hello, boys,” she said. Lulu was surprised that she was using a friendly voice with the people who were poaching on her land.

Mike and Tommy came up the steps. “Hi, Ms. Wiggins,” he said. “This is my friend, Tommy Rand.”

Tommy put out his hand to shake hands with Ms. Wiggins. “It’s a pleasure to meet you,” he said.

Lulu had never seen Tommy Rand and Mike Lacey act like gentlemen. What a joke!

“We want to talk to you about something, Ms. Wiggins,” said Mike.

“I’m pleased you’ve come to see me on your own,” Ms. Wiggins said. She motioned to the three girls on the porch behind her. "You know these girls, I'm sure."

"Yeah," said Tommy. "We know them."

Ms. Wiggins motioned to some empty chairs. "Sit down, boys. I'll pour you some lemonade."

Lulu was shocked that Ms. Wiggins was being so nice to Mike and Tommy. She could see that Anna and Pam were surprised, too. Why was Ms. Wiggins treating Tommy and Mike like friends instead of criminals?

On the Porch

"We want to talk to you alone," Mike told Ms. Wiggins.

"The girls can stay," said Ms. Wiggins. "We're talking about something that concerns them. They're worried about the safety of the animals in my woods. So am I."

Tommy shot a mean look at the Pony Pals. "I told you they were tattletales," he said to Mike.

"Boys, what is it you have to tell me?" asked Ms. Wiggins.

"We put traps on your land," Mike said.

"But we didn't catch anything," added Tommy.

"The traps didn't work," explained Mike.

Anna and Lulu exchanged a quick smile.

"Why didn't they work?" asked Ms. Wiggins.

Tommy glared at the Pony Pals. "Because they messed with them," he said. "They're running all over your woods with those horses."

"They're not *horses,*" said Pam. "They're *ponies.*"

"The girls have permission to ride their ponies on the trails," said Ms. Wiggins. "And last week I told you, Mike, that you could ride your bike there. But no one has permission to trap. Did I forget to tell you that, Mike?"

Mike looked at his feet. "No, ma'am," he said. "You didn't forget."

"How did you boys learn how to trap?" Ms. Wiggins asked.

Tommy pointed to Mike. "Mike said he knew how. And he had all these traps."

"How did you learn, Mike?" asked Ms. Wiggins.

Lulu thought Ms. Wiggins was being too nice to Mike and Tommy. She looked at Pam and rolled her eyes.

"My father taught me how to trap," Mike said. "We used to do it together. But with permits and everything legal."

What father? Lulu wondered. She knew that Mike lived with his mother and sister.

"Why don't you trap with your father anymore?" asked Ms. Wiggins.

"He's not here," answered Mike.

"His dad left town," said Tommy. "So his folks got divorced."

Mike shot an angry look at Tommy. "I can tell it myself," he said. "My dad lives in Chicago," Mike continued. "He's got an apartment there. He gave me the traps. They were like a present from him."

Lulu felt the camera in her pocket and

remembered how her dad had given it to her.

Tommy laughed. "Your dad just left those traps behind," he said. "What was he going to do with traps in Chicago? Catch squirrels in the park?"

Mike glared at Tommy. "Shut up about my father," he hissed.

Ms. Wiggins glared at Tommy, too. "Do you understand why I don't allow trapping on my land?" Ms. Wiggins asked him.

"Because you like all the animals," said Tommy.

"I also want people to be free to use the land without worrying about someone — or some pony — being caught by a trap," she said.

"Are you going to tell on us?" Tommy asked Ms. Wiggins.

"Should I?" Ms. Wiggins asked.

"Yes!" the Pony Pals said in unison.

Tommy shot a mean look at the Pony

Pals. "Mind your own business," he said. "This isn't your property."

"I'm sorry I trapped on your land," Mike told Ms. Wiggins. "I was just trying to make some money."

"Money for what?" asked Ms. Wiggins.

"For a plane ticket to Chicago," said Mike.

"You want to go to Chicago to see your father?" asked Ms. Wiggins.

Mike nodded.

"Do you like trapping?" Ms. Wiggins asked Tommy.

"It's boring. Besides, I'm going to summer camp in two days."

"Are you going to camp, Mike?" Ms. Wiggins asked.

Mike shook his head. Lulu knew that Mike couldn't go to sleep-away camp because it was too expensive.

"Maybe you would like a job working for me," said Ms. Wiggins. "I need someone to help Mr. Silver clean up the trails."

Mike broke into a smile. “You mean I’d get paid?” he asked.

“Yes,” she said. “If Mr. Silver says you’re a good worker.”

“Can we go now?” asked Tommy.

“I’ll walk you to your bikes,” said Ms. Wiggins. “We have to discuss how I’m going to handle this matter with your parents.”

Ms. Wiggins went down the porch steps with Mike and Tommy. Lulu couldn’t hear what she was saying.

“How come she gave Mike a job?” asked Pam.

“She feels sorry for him because of his dad being gone,” said Anna.

“I know how that feels,” said Lulu.

Ms. Wiggins came back on the porch. The boys were already halfway down the driveway. Ms. Wiggins sighed. “Well,” she said, “that’s taken care of.” She gave the girls a nice smile. “We’ve found our poachers, thanks to you. You girls did great detective

work. Who knows how many animals' lives you've saved."

A few minutes later the girls walked over to the paddock to get the ponies. It was time to go back to their campsite. Ms. Wiggins walked with them. When they reached the paddock, Ms. Wiggins asked, "Lulu can I use your camera to take a picture of the Pony Pal Detectives?"

"That'd be great," said Anna.

"We'll stand near the gate," said Pam.

Lulu handed Ms. Wiggins the camera. "If it's a picture of the Pony Pal Detectives," Lulu said, "Snow White should be in it, too. She helped solve this case."

Everyone agreed. Lulu called to her pony, and Snow White ran over to the gate. The Pony Pals posed for the photo. Lulu put her arms around her pony and whispered, "Snow White, you're terrific!"

Ms. Wiggins snapped their picture.

Dear Reader,

I am having a lot of fun researching and writing books about the Pony Pals. I've met many interesting kids and adults who love ponies. And I've visited some wonderful ponies at homes, farms, and riding schools.

Before writing Pony Pals I wrote fourteen novels for children and young adults. Four of these were honored by Children's Choice Awards.

I live in Sharon, Connecticut, with my husband, Lee, and our dog, Willie. Our daughter is all grown up and has her own apartment in New York City.

Besides writing novels I like to draw, paint, garden and swim. I didn't have a pony when I was growing up, but I have always loved them and dreamt about riding. Now I take riding lessons on a horse named Saz. To learn more, visit my Web site: www.jeannebetancourt.com.

I like reading and writing about ponies as much as I do riding. Which proves to me that you don't have to ride a pony to love them. And you certainly don't need a pony to be a Pony Pal.

Happy Reading,

Jeanne Betancourt